What His Father Did

What His Father Did

Jacqueline Dembar Greene

Illustrated by John O'Brien

Houghton Mifflin Company
Boston   1992

For Dad, who led me along the way to Minsk
—J. D. G.

For Tess
—J. O'B.

Library of Congress Cataloging-in-Publication Data

Greene, Jacqueline Dembar.
    What his father did / Jacqueline D. Greene ; {illustrated by John O'Brien}.
        p.   cm.
    Summary: A crafty beggar tricks an innkeeper into giving him a free dinner by threatening to do what the beggar's father did when he got no dinner.
    ISBN 0-395-55042-4
    {1. Folklore, Jewish.} I. O'Brien, John, 1953- ill. II. Title.
PZ8.1.G835Wh   1991   91-16254
398.21—dc20   CIP
                                AC

Printed in the United States of America

HOR   10   9   8   7   6   5   4   3   2   1

Whenever the villagers gathered to entertain each other with stories, there were always tales to be told about Herschel's pranks. Herschel was a poor man, but what he lacked in silver kopeks he more than made up for in cleverness. He could trick the greatest of misers into giving him whatever he needed, and everyone respected his boldness and wit.

One morning Herschel learned that his elderly aunt in the village of Pinsk was ill. "I must visit her," he decided. "But how can I travel all the way from Minsk to Pinsk with just one lonely kopek in my pocket?"

Then Herschel remembered a cozy inn halfway between the two villages, in the tiny town of Linsk. If I keep my wits about me, he thought, perhaps one kopek will be exactly enough. And he set off upon the dusty road.

Herschel hitched a ride on a hay wagon, then begged a ride on a milk cart, and finally used his own feet.

It was night when he reached the inn. His feet ached and his stomach growled, for he had eaten nothing all day. He entered and banged loudly on the table.

"Innkeeper! Innkeeper!" he shouted. A short, round woman hurried into the room, wiping her hands on her apron.

"I am the innkeeper," she said. "What can I do for you?"

"How much for a bed for the night?" he demanded.

Her face crinkled into a smile, and she smoothed her hair toward the tight little bun on the top of her head. "For the finest, cleanest room, and the softest, warmest bed," she cooed, "just three kopeks."

"Outrageous!" thundered Herschel.

The innkeeper held up her hand as if to stop a charging bull. "Wait!" she commanded. "If you cannot afford a bed, you may sleep in the finest, cleanest hay, in the freshest, airiest loft, for just two kopeks!"

"Robbery!" roared Herschel.

The innkeeper sighed. "All right then," she said. "If you cannot afford to sleep in the barn, this is my last offer. You may sleep on the shiniest, smoothest floor for just one kopek!"

"Is the floor in front of the fireplace?" asked Herschel.

"For you—the fireplace!" said the woman.

"Agreed!" said Herschel. He took the kopek from his pocket and slapped it on the table. "And now, innkeeper, bring me some supper! You are looking at a starving man."

The woman looked the traveler up and down. He did indeed look starved. His clothes were in tatters and his boots were full of holes. She guessed that the man had just spent his last kopek and now expected to trick her into giving him supper.

"In truth," she said, "there isn't a crumb left to eat."

"Curses!" shouted Herschel. "How can a man walk from Minsk to Linsk to Pinsk on an empty stomach?" He set his mouth in a hideous frown, plunked himself into a chair, and folded his arms. "That settles it! If you will give me nothing to eat, I shall have to do what my father did when he was given no supper!"

The woman's bun unraveled. "What, pray tell, did your father do?" she asked in a trembling voice.

"That is for me to know," said Herschel. "But this I will say—he did it more than once!"

The woman was worried. Who would hear her if she cried for help? The other guests were fast asleep upstairs. Perhaps the man's father was a thief—or worse!

"Wait!" she said quickly. "The baker's house is not far. There's a chance he may yet have a loaf of bread." And she hurried out without another word.

In no time, she was rapping at the baker's door. The startled baker yelled from the window, "Who is it at this late hour?"

"It's me, the innkeeper," she said, "and I need your help. There's a raggedy vagabond at the inn, and I'm sure he hasn't a kopek to his name. He says he can't travel from Minsk to Linsk to Pinsk on an empty stomach, and if I don't feed him supper, he'll just have to do what his father did! What shall I do?"

"Why, his father may have been a thief—or worse!" said the baker. "You must save your neck. Look at it this way, it can't hurt to give a bit of charity to a poor traveler." So the baker handed down his last loaf of bread, and would accept nothing in return except the innkeeper's thanks. She tucked the bread under her arm and bustled away.

But the woman did not know if a loaf of bread was enough, so she
decided to stop at the cheese seller's house. She knocked on the door so
hard that the big sign overhead began to sway and creak.

"Who's knocking down my door at this hour?" shouted the cheese seller.

"It's the innkeeper," the woman said, "and I need your help."

The door opened, and the cheese seller listened as the innkeeper told her tale. "There's a raggedy vagabond at the inn, and I'm sure he hasn't a kopek to his name. He says he can't travel from Minsk to Linsk to Pinsk on an empty stomach, and if I don't feed him supper he'll have to do what his father did. What shall I do?"

"You poor woman," cried the cheese seller. "There's no telling what kind of dangerous man his father may have been. You must think of your own safety."

So she cut off a large slice of cheese, fetched a pail of goat's milk, and wrapped up a few blintzes that were left over from her own supper. These she offered to the innkeeper, and would accept nothing in return. The woman thanked her and hurried away.

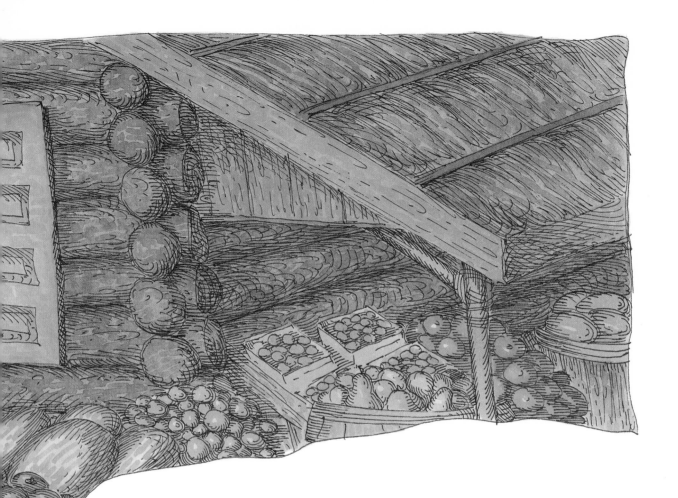

Still she was not certain that she had enough food for the traveler. Just to be sure, she walked to the fruit peddler's house and kicked sharply at the door.

The fruit peddler's head appeared at the window, and he held out a candle to see who was at his door.

"It's the innkeeper," called the woman, "and I need your help. There's a raggedy vagabond at the inn, and I'm sure he hasn't a kopek to his name. He says that he can't travel from Minsk to Linsk to Pinsk on an empty stomach, and if I don't feed him supper, he'll do what his father did. What shall I do?"

The fruit peddler appeared at the door holding a basket of apples and grapes.

"Oh, mercy!" he croaked. "Who knows what manner of rogue or robber his father may have been? You must feed the man well. But look at it this way, only good can come of helping a poor traveler. Here is some fruit that is too ripe to sell."

"Grateful thanks," said the woman. "You may have saved my life."
And she hurried back to the inn.

When she entered, Herschel was still seated in the chair with his arms folded across his chest. But his frown had been replaced by a look of expectation.

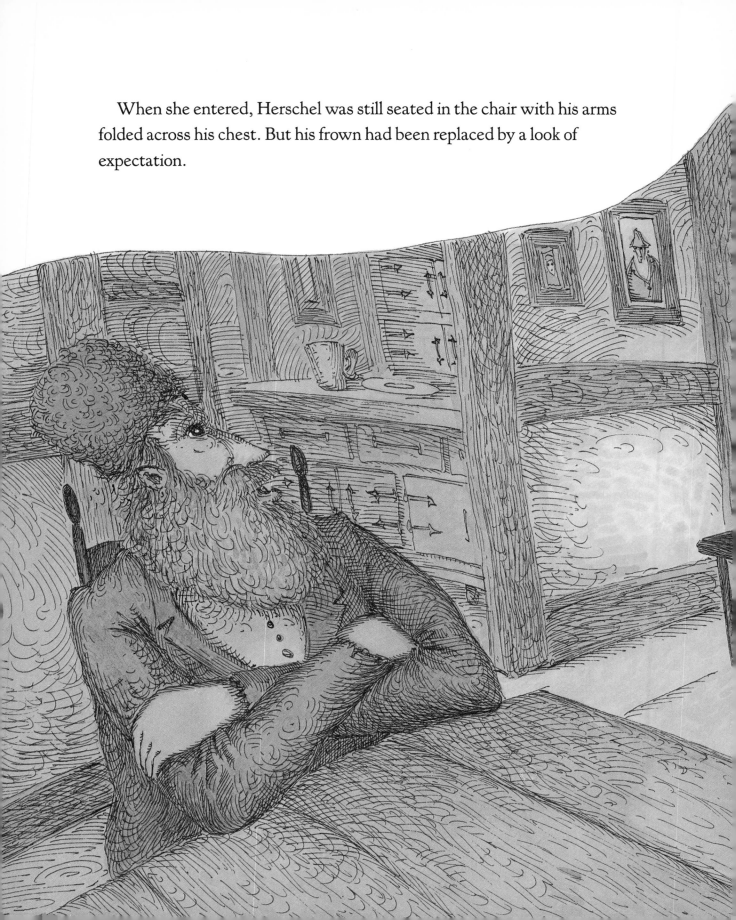

"Come and eat," said the innkeeper to Herschel, as she set out all the things she had gathered.

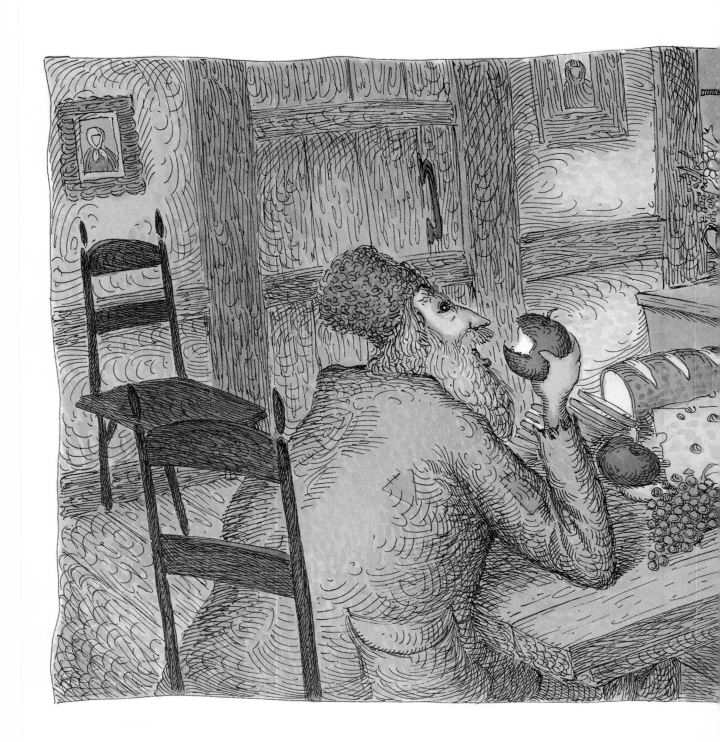

She spread the bread and the cheese, the goat's milk and the blintzes, the apples and the grapes before him on the table.

Herschel ate every bit of food, except for two apples, which he boldly stuffed into his pockets. "Thank you, my good woman," he said. "Now I shall not have to do what my father did when he was given no supper!"

The woman heaved a sigh of relief. "Thank goodness!" she said. "But, good sir, you must tell me what it was your father did."

Herschel curled up on the floor in front of the fire, and as he
closed his eyes, he said, "Well, naturally, my father went to bed with
an empty stomach! And believe me, he did it more than once!"

DATE			